About the Author

I was born and raised in central London and spent most of my adult life there. I also lived in Spain for a couple of years and now live in Suffolk. I love travelling and discovering new places; I should have made holidaying a career! I have a busy, active life and love writing stories; always have done, really. I like to see the characters come to life; I get withdrawal symptoms if I haven't got a good book on the go. I'm also learning guitar (slowly) but my biggest achievements are definitely my two wonderful sons.

A Little Book of Short Stories

Bev Sargeant

A Little Book of Short Stories

Olympia Publishers
London

www.olympiapublishers.com
OLYMPIA PAPERBACK EDITION

A CIP catalogue record for this title is
available from the British Library.

ISBN: 978-1-80074-416-5

This is a work of fiction.
Names, characters, places and incidents originate from the writer's
imagination. Any resemblance to actual persons, living or dead, is
purely coincidental.

First Published in 2021

Olympia Publishers
Tallis House
2 Tallis Street
London
EC4Y 0AB

Printed in Great Britain

Dedication

To Louis and Daniel, whom I love more than words
could ever say.

WAITING

Annie stood there by her front gate watching, almost like it was in slow motion, the sudden frenzied activity along her street. Her tiny cul de sac, containing only eight houses, was now alive with cars, vans and people she had never seen before, shouting instructions to each other over loudspeakers.

There were a number of people in police uniform and Annie had been told by quite a fierce woman with a clipboard to just wait by her gate and someone would come and talk to her. To be honest, her tone was really rather rude, and in the circumstances, not at all calming. That had been over an hour ago. Annie was now feeling very anxious and kept going over and over in her head what she knew she had to say.

Annie looked down at the dowdy green dressing gown she had on, which looked like someone had just thrown a bowl of mushy peas down her. Why did she have to be wearing this! Yes, not a good look and her hair, well, what a disaster that looked. There had been no time, they had said, but here she still stood waiting.

Annie was thirty-two years old, with long, curly, dark blonde hair, green eyes, tall, slim and usually, when she was not looking how she did today, was very striking-looking and turned many a man's, and indeed woman's, head when she walked down the street.

Annie didn't wear much make-up; she didn't need to. She was one of those very lucky women who had flawless, fresh-looking skin, although the colour green of the dressing gown was not doing her looks any favours today.

As a child Annie dreamed of becoming a famous ice skater, as she loved to skate. In fact, aside from ice skating, which she discovered in her early teens, from when she was about six her Jacko roller skates seemed to become part of her feet, skating about everywhere. She had also quite liked the idea of becoming an actor, which seemed fitting with her always seeking to be centre of attention.

As she stood there waiting, Annie thought about how life just sweeps you along sometimes with your dreams lying dormant, gathering dust. She couldn't say she was unhappy; she just felt unfulfilled, like something was missing. At thirty-two, were her dreams still achievable? Well, probably not being a famous ice skater.

Annie looked across at the detached white bungalow, with two chimneys either end of the roof which had probably been blocked off some years ago: in the winter there was never any smoke coming from them, which was a bit of a relief, considering a family of jackdaws seemed to have taken up permanent residence in them; actually, more like two families, one in each chimney.

Annie could see Mr and Mrs Peacock, who were both in their seventies and had lived there for years and always took a keen interest in everyone's business, crouching down by the window, trying to covertly watch everything going on in the street. Quite comical really, thought Annie and let out a little laugh, which slightly eased the tension she was feeling, as there was no way they couldn't be seen in their matching bright orange jumpers.

Mr and Mrs Peacock had attempted to come outside, with their eyes darting everywhere and craning their necks to see all that was going on. Clipboard fierce lady soon put a stop to that though, and ushered them back inside as she loudly and very abruptly told them they really could only allow those involved to be outside on the street.

The paramedics had arrived now and instructions were again bellowing from the loudspeakers. A van that had been obscuring Annie's full view of the street moved further back, and then Annie saw him and her stomach did somersaults and she felt physically sick.

The man was about thirty, with long dark hair, wearing a white t-shirt and dark jeans, his left arm completely covered in a tattoo of a horse with wings, Pegasus no doubt. His body was motionless and the blood was running down from the top of his head and covering his white t-shirt. Annie was shaking and so desperately needed someone to give her a big hug to calm her, but there was no time.

Annie saw the person who she knew was in charge walking towards her and she knew she had to get a grip. This was important as she had to get it right and say what she had been rehearsing in her head; she had to be believable, this was her chance and she couldn't muck it up.

The man spoke to Annie in a very authoritative but calm manner, explaining exactly what they needed from her. Annie looked over to where she had been instructed to go and steadily walked towards the man lying on the ground surrounded by police and paramedics.

Annie's heart was beating so fast and loud she was sure everyone around her, even Mr and Mrs Peacock banished inside, could hear it. Her palms were sweaty and as she looked around, there were what felt like a million eyes intently staring at her. She gulped, closed her eyes for a second and took a very deep breath.

The loudspeaker boomed out its instructions, full lights beamed all around and Annie then ran so fast that the police were unable to stop her before she threw her arms around the man on the floor, screaming hysterically, "No no not my John, please, please, someone help him." The loudspeaker boomed again, "That's a rap, break for lunch," and everyone started clapping. Wow, her first speaking part as an extra on this film and with the luck of the location being on her own street Annie was so pleased, she had done it word perfect with no retakes. Waiting was a pain, but Annie felt so happy with her own small achievement and knew she would look forward to the next waiting around time she would no doubt have to endure as a regular film extra.

COSMIC WONDER

Sitting alone on the hill, Cathy wrapped her arms around herself and gazed up at the night sky, full of bright shining stars that on this clear night seemed so close she could almost touch them.

Cathy had always felt drawn to the stars and the moon ever since she was a child, as they seemed to calm her when she felt stressed or upset. As a child, whenever she had been naughty and sent to her room by her parents, usually following a temper tantrum, she would lie in her bed by the window, pull back the curtains and stare at the sky. Whilst the moon or stars were not always visible, just knowing they were there among the vast darkness of the sky felt like a warm comfort blanket soothing her. Tonight, after the sad events of the day she needed to feel the calming influence of the celestial sky once again.

Cathy spent nearly every summer at her gran's, whose house was perched high on a hill overlooking the town, with the church steeple peeking over a row of white terrace houses which were just beside the river. The house was painted pink, had four latticed windows at the front, a sturdy brown oak door with a wooden knocker and wide letterbox and a thatched roof. From a distance it looked like a welcoming, smiling face.

Cathy's gran loved to bake and was always happy to share her cakes with her neighbours and their children, so during those summers there were always lots of visitors and plenty of other children for Cathy to play with.

At the end of those long, hot summer days, Cathy would sit outside on the top of that hill with her gran and count the stars and talk and talk about what wonderful mysteries the universe may hold.

Her gran had always been such a free spirit, and as a child, had dreamt of travelling to far-off places she had read about in books, which held such charm and mystery. As an adult, as part of her job as a newspaper journalist she had indeed been lucky enough to visit so many incredible places and oh, what wonderful stories she had to tell from her many travels, stories Cathy loved to hear and could listen to for hours on end.

Aside from current affairs, her gran had a fascination with the universe and what lay beyond the vastness. She definitely made Cathy's thoughts spiral when she would say, "OK, so at the end of the immense darkness, many planets and bright twinkling stars, there could just be a brick wall, but what is beyond the brick wall? Maybe it's just never-ending."

Tonight, as Cathy sat there on that same hill staring up at the magical sky, she thought about the day and the many times she and her gran had sat in the same spot. Whilst she felt such terrible sadness and pain at the loss of her gran, she felt comforted by the wonderful, large turnout of people at her gran's funeral, as this showed she was loved so very much.

Looking at the amazing planetary night sky, she imagined her gran now becoming part of the whole cosmic wonder.

THROUGH A STRANGER'S EYES

Jay was twenty-six years old, or that's what he thought was the case, having attempted to work it out by the phases of the moon and the sun. He had dark, curly hair, brown eyes and a lean, tanned body which was probably due to always being out in the open, either working on the land or fishing.

Jay had been living on this remote island from as far back as he could remember, where people lived a very simple life "living off the fruits of the gods", as one of the older inhabitants would chant as part of his daily ritual down by the water's edge.

Jay had come to accept this life but always felt something was missing, and most recently had become very curious as to what might lay beyond the sea's horizon or even what mysteries the moon and sun held.

Jay was a very kind and thoughtful young man and was thankful for the food, which came from the natural sources growing on the island and the fish in the sea, and shelter made of wood from the many trees. He had great respect for the people he had grown up amongst and embraced their gentle and kind ways. However, his life was feeling very unfulfilled and to be blunt he was bored and inside was screaming for some excitement. Surely there had to be something else, thought Jay.

Jay couldn't recall anyone ever visiting the island, so all he knew was what he was taught by the islanders. The islanders' lifestyle and daily activities revolved around the rising and setting of the sun and wonderful phases of the moon.

Jay stood at the water's edge, staring out at the vastness in front of him, letting the waves gently cascade around his feet. He did once ask one of the elders whether the island was near to any other civilisation. His question was met with a stony silence, although the elder's wife, before she could be hushed, blurted out something about a metropolis named New York, where they had originally dwelled before they were fortunate enough to find the island. New York, New York, Jay said. He liked the sound of that.

The sun was still high in the sky, so Jay knew sunset was still a long way off. As he continued to stare out to sea, he could see a large object moving in the water, which initially he believed to be a fish, but then he heard a sound coming from the object, like a whirring sound. As he looked closer, it wasn't a fish but a boat moving quite fast towards the shore. Jay felt a thrill of excitement run through him at the prospect of meeting new people and what tales they might have of other sights and places.

As the boat got nearer, he could see it was occupied by a man and woman with a small boy, who looked like he had been crying. The man called out to Jay, "Are we anywhere near New York? We seem to have lost our bearings on our way back from Long Island." Jay was mesmerised: that name again, he thought, New York. The man thought Jay hadn't heard him, so he repeated his question. Jay's mind was reeling as he knew this was his chance to seek the adventure his soul was craving. He told the man that if he would allow him on board he was sure he could help them get back to New York. The man agreed, and without any hesitation Jay climbed aboard and off they went in search of New York New York.

Jay established that the family had only been off-track for about ten minutes and they had come from a westerly direction, which meant that this metropolis was not far. Jay was very familiar with navigating when fishing in his tiny makeshift shaft using the sun as a compass, and as such to the relief of the family and the almost uncontrollable joy of Jay, land was soon visible in front of them.

As they got nearer, Jay stared in awe at the tall buildings that seemed to rise from the water and disappear high into the clouds above the skyline. Oh, my oh my, said Jay, this is a metropolis.

The family were so grateful and insisted on taking Jay to meet their friends and family, who were having a Halloween party; they would take him back safely to his island the following day. Jay had no idea what Halloween was, but he was excited to find out. Let the adventure begin, thought Jay.

There were sounds and wonderful smells all around Jay that he had never experienced before, and several times on the way to where the family had parked what they stated was their Range Rover, Jay stopped to take in all of his surroundings.

There were crowds of people everywhere and

everyone seemed in such a hurry, bustling each other out of the way. Jay started to feel a bit anxious and when he turned back in the direction the family were heading, he couldn't see them. Jay suddenly felt scared. He called out the man's name, which he had discovered was Tim, but there was no sign of them and it dawned on Jay that when he had stopped to view his surroundings, he may have started to head off in the opposite direction to the family.

Jay looked up at the sun, which by now was very low, almost touching the water. Oh no, what was he to do? At that moment he felt really bad as he knew his fellow islanders would be looking for him and they would be worried.

Without even realising it, Jay started to walk away from the bright lights of the harbour, mainly being pushed along by the crowds. Before he knew it, he found himself in a street with brown stone buildings with metal steps on the side leading from the ground to the roof.

Jay jumped slightly when suddenly there was a lot of angry shouting, which was coming from the window of one of the brown stone buildings. Jay had never heard two people shout in such an unfriendly, aggressive way and he now started to feel that he had found a very hostile place, which made him feel very uneasy and even more desperate to find Tim and his family.

Jay looked for the sun to guide him back to the harbour, but sunset had been and gone. Suddenly Jay heard a roar of excitement and coming towards him was the scariest thing he had ever seen. He was so terrified he couldn't move.

In front of and all around him were strange creatures, some small and some tall. His bible readings had described such images and now here they were, standing in front of him in all their horror, devils both small and large, with huge red horns and long pointed tails, witches with their broomsticks, so ugly you daren't look them in the eyes, and green goblin-type figures looking very menacing.

Jay watched in fear as in turn they walked up the steps of the brown stone buildings and banged on the doors shouting, "Trick or treat." People came out and willingly handed over whatever it was these hideous beings wanted, which Jay assumed was to avoid whatever "trick" they may bestow on them if they did not obey them. Jay needed to get away before they saw him as he had nothing to appease them with.

Jay ran back in the direction he had come, bumping into more creatures, all carrying bags that would soon be filled with their ill-gotten gains. Jay needed to stop to catch his breath and as he did, the most grotesque thing he had ever seen, with green slime foaming from his mouth, touched him on the shoulder and leered, "Trick or treat." Jay literally collapsed with shock.

Jay came to and slowly opened his eyes. The first thing he saw was the starlit sky and he thought how beautiful it looked. A figure was standing over him that looked vaguely familiar; then Jay recognised Tim, whom he could have hugged as he was so pleased to see him. Tim said, "Jay, we were worried about you and thought we had lost you; you seem to have had a bit of a fall." Tim stretched out his hand to help Jay up and at that moment, the slimy green thing appeared over Tim's left shoulder.

Jay was speechless and began to shake with terror. Tim looked confused, then looked over his shoulder and laughed and said, "Oh I see you've met my brother." Oh no, thought Jay, Tim was one of them, disguised as a human. It was hopeless; he would not get out of this alive and running, he knew, would be futile.

Tim was now quite concerned and said, "Jay, whatever is wrong, buddy? You look absolutely terrified." The slimy creature started to move and then laughing, removed the green face, saying, "Wow, this must be the best costume ever, the way it's clearly spooked you." Jay couldn't believe it as he was looking into the exact same face as Tim's. Tim said, "Jay, this is my twin brother Tom, who is just a big kid on Halloween."

They took Jay back to the family home, carefully explaining along the way about the festival of Halloween and the meaning behind trick and treat. Never having experienced anything like it in his life Jay was confused, but realised these were kind, good people and had no intention of hurting him.

As agreed, Jay stayed the night with the family and even joined in on their Halloween games of retrieving the apple out of a bucket of water with just your mouth. All the children really were adorable and Jay, once he felt relaxed and safe, so enjoyed the time he spent with Tim and his family.

As promised, the next day Tim took Jay back to the island. While Tim said that he would come back and take

Jay back for another trip one day, Jay knew that as much as he had eventually enjoyed his visit to the big metropolis, New York was way too fast and loud for him.

Jay would always treasure his adventure but his life on the island was exactly what his soul needed. He loved the gentle, unassuming lifestyle, where everyone knew the role they needed to play, as dwellers of this wonderful island, which gave them all a sense of peace and belonging.

One day, thought Jay, when he became an elder, he may well share the details of the sights, smells and people he had once had the pleasure to come across during a time so long ago, in a strange and noisy land across the sea.

A TOUCH OF SUSPENSE

George slowly opened his eyes, which was a struggle as he felt like he had been in a comatose sleep for a long time. His mouth felt dry and his head was sore, banging along to the beat of an invisible marching band which had taken up residence there.

George was trying to focus on what the hell happened last night, which he was finding hard to do with the marching band competing with his memory for his attention. His mind was very fuzzy; fragments of the previous night started to flash before his eyes, but these were still very hazy.

George sat up slowly and whilst the room he was in was pitch black, he knew instinctively that this was not his bedroom. As he swung his legs off the bed and onto the floor, his bare feet touched a cold, tiled surface, which definitely confirmed that he was not at home, as his bedroom floor was covered with the most voluptuous soft carpet, which seemed to massage your feet as you walked on it.

George stretched out his hands in search of a bedside light, but there was just empty space. He stood up with his arms out in front of him, found what felt like a wall and again searched for a light switch, without success.

George stood still for a moment, wondering where the hell he was. Then he suddenly heard a loud and somewhat creepy dripping sound, which sounded like it was coming from right in front of him.

George edged slowly towards the ominous dripping sound. His heart was beating fast and his forehead felt hot and sweaty, with his thoughts again on the previous night's activities.

George truly wished he had just gone straight home after work and not popped along for "one drink", which as he knew only too well always led to well in excess of ten, plus leaving him with the inevitable hangover from hell the next day. When would he learn!

As George stood there in the dark, feeling slightly afraid and vulnerable, he reflected on the night before and how an after-work catch up down the pub had turned sinister. Everyone had been in good spirits and although there was the usual banter, this was light-hearted. Yes, they had all probably drunk far too much, but everyone was laughing and happy.

However, the mood changed when a young girl ran into the pub, distraught and shouting for help. Tears were rolling down her face and she was shaking uncontrollably and pointing out into the street. A few people ran to the door, but George got there first and saw a young man with blonde hair wearing a white t-shirt and dark jeans, holding what looked like a woman's handbag. George heard the girl shout, "He took my bag", so George lunged towards the young man with the intention of grabbing the bag. Due to his excessive alcohol consumption, George's coordination was way off and instead his elbow hit the man hard in the nose.

The man was screaming, "He's broke my nose", and blood was dripping down his white t-shirt. George had also slipped during the scuffle and hurt his head. Someone had already called the police and when they arrived, onlookers were pointing the finger of blame right at George.

Back in the dark room George moved further towards the dripping sound, which had now become heavier and then suddenly light flooded the room, causing George to cover his eyes with his hands. He could now hear various voices and blinking, his eyes adjusting to the onslaught of light, George in that instant knew exactly where he was and why.

The sight that confronted George was the dripping sound of a shower beyond a glass partition and unbelievably, among several other men, he also saw the same young man he had had an altercation with outside the pub. He looked at the cold, tiled floor beneath his feet, the shelf with a worn, shabby mattress and the iron-barred door, and the arrest of the night before all came back to him like a hard smack around the face.

It came to light that the police had been looking for the young man for previous offences of bag snatching and he was arrested. George was also taken to the cells but only for being drunk and disorderly, as witnesses had supported George's statement that he had only intended to try and retrieve the bag.

It wasn't long before a uniformed officer came to open George's cell and advised him that he was free to go, and that he could pick up his belongings from the desk sergeant.

George was relieved as he couldn't wait to get home, have a nice hot shower and crawl into his own lovely, comfortable bed.

That was a night George would not forget in a long time and he vowed to never drink again; well, until the next time!

THE JOURNEY CONTINUES

Rachel looked at her watch., which flashed 10.37 a.m. She couldn't believe that was all the time was, as she had set off just after nine a.m. and it felt like she'd been walking for hours. She took off her backpack, which was pretty rubbish and was definitely not as it was advertised, as being "deluxe and comfortable". That it most certainly was not, as the straps had started to rub against her shoulders and even through her jacket! Something her mum always used to say sprung to mind, "Buy cheap, buy twice." Yes, you were sure right there, mum, Rachel thought.

Rachel sat down on the grass bank overlooking the stream which rippled down from the mountain waterfall, on its journey towards the waiting river a few miles ahead. "Damn it"; the flipping grass was damp and now she had a wet bottom to go with her aching shoulders, and feet, come to think of it.

Rachel's mood was starting to dip into the dangerously low zone, a place she had been many times before, which she called her dark hole. She didn't want to be in that place of mind, but without warning it sometimes just crept up on her and dragged her in. When this happened there was nothing she could do; she just had to ride with it until the heavy feeling of sadness and despair slowly ebbed away.

Rachel by now knew the score in this respect, having been there many times before, so was fully aware that it wouldn't last long and she would soon come out the other side, back into the light. She took out her water bottle, took a sip and forced her mind to think back to happier times when she thought she was the luckiest woman alive.

Rachel had indeed been very lucky. She had married a man she had loved so very deeply and who loved her back tenfold. Rachel and her husband both worked hard and landed themselves good jobs that paid well. They went on to have two wonderful boys whom they both cherished; yes, they really had it all. Sadly, Rachel's idyllic world was soon about to crumble.

Rachel's mother-in-law had been diagnosed with cancer, which was very aggressive and sadly the doctors were not very hopeful. Her husband, and of course Rachel, were devastated. Her husband, being an only child, was really close to his mum and he adored her, and during that terrible time he was with his mum every step of the way.

Two days before Rachel's mother-in-law lost her battle with the dreaded disease, Rachel's dad was suddenly rushed to hospital with excruciating pains in his foot and leg, which were due to a blood clot: it travelled to his brain, killing him instantly. Rachel's dad and her husband's mum died within two days of each other, both far too young at the age of sixty. Rachel and her husband's world fell apart.

The years and life rolled on, but now always tinged with sadness. Rachel and her husband's relationship, was stronger than ever; their boys were growing fast and both doing well in school and then… whack, another bomb exploded!

Rachel's husband was diagnosed with a rare autoimmune disease. He fought the good fight for three years but then caught pneumonia and had a massive heart attack and died on Valentine's Day. Rachel howled like a wounded animal for days until she slipped into a complete state of depression. It was only the thought of her boys also being without a mum too that gave her the strength to go on and be strong. It was a daily uphill struggle but eventually with the help of her boys, mum and friends, the dark days started to get further and further apart.

Again, the earth kept revolving and Rachel kept herself busy at work and spending quality time with her family and friends. She again felt lucky to have such wonderful support around her and she cherished her family and friends so much.

Rachel had always been really close to her mum and when her mum became ill, Rachel became her carer, and was with her holding her hand, stroking her hair and singing one of her mum's favourite songs to her when she peacefully passed away in the early hours of a cold and rainy October morning. Rachel felt so alone, and the dark days again became a frequent visitor.

Rachel looked around her as she sat on that grassy bank and could hear her mum saying, "There is so much beauty in this world; look around you, life really is worth living. Get out there, do what you really want to do, face your challenges."

"Yes, you are so right," said Rachel out loud, "life is precious and a privilege, and today I'm facing my challenge to climb the highest peak. I'm doing that for my dad, my husband and my mum, who, if they were still among the living would say, "Don't waste another day."

MARKET LIFE

Jim rubbed his hands together, trying to create some heat as he stood behind his market stall on a cold and bleak February morning. It was still quite early and as he looked around, other stallholders were still setting up and getting ready to sell their many different wares, from ladies' fashions, household cleaning items, retro music, handcrafted wooden ornaments and children's clothes to fruit and veg.

Jim looked up at the depressing, gloomy grey sky, which he felt very aptly matched his mood. He hated days like this when the dreary weather would no doubt result in a poor turnout, as who would really want to be browsing market stalls, freezing their butts off, when nowadays most things were readily available in the nice, warm, big supermarkets? Jim sighed loudly which caught the attention of Harry, who had the market stall next to him.

"You all right Jim?" said Harry.

"Yeah, mate," said Jim, "just hate this damn weather and just know today's gonna be a slow one."

"You're not wrong there, mate, bring back the good old days when people came to the market come rain or shine. What happened 'ay, Jim, what the hell happened?"

Jim had worked the market from way back when he was a young lad, helping his dad, Reg, who likewise had also started out the same way when he was a lad. Yep, they were a family of market traders through and through, selling all kinds of household items from oven gloves to kitchen bins. Basically, anything you needed in that respect, they sold it, and if they didn't have it on the day, they'd happily order it for you.

The glory days were when the market was such a lively, energetic place, where people came not just to shop but for the experience. The bargains, the brightly coloured stalls, the entertaining market traders capturing the crowd's attention with their wisecracks and theatrics, the wonderful smells of what then seemed like exotic food from the market street cafe, the laughter and banter between the stallholders and how they always seemed to make their customers who frequented the many stalls feel part of their vibrant world. Yes, people came because the liveliness and the familiar friendly characters gave them a sense of being part of something, a community which was theirs and where they felt safe.

Jim continued rubbing his hands and thought about those days gone by, remembering how he used to so look forward to getting to the market each day. Oh yes, back in the day as far as he was concerned it was the best job ever and he considered himself very fortunate. When did it all change though, as it was not fun any more, just a daily struggle to survive and make ends meet?

In his heyday, at six feet, slim built with broad shoulders, dark brown hair and the bluest sparkling eyes ever seen, he was very popular with all the girls who visited the market. They'd stop at his stall and buy anything just to get his attention. Jim was always polite but for all his good looks he was really rather shy, so when a pretty girl gave him the eye, he just got embarrassed and tongue-tied and never really said much to them, which of course made him all the more attractive. Although, there was one girl he had had his eye on for some time.

Opposite Jim and Reg's stall was a costume jewellery stall selling handmade bracelets made from different coloured beads with matching earrings. The stall owner and jewellery maker, was an attractive lady called Stella, who was in her mid-forties and had the most loud, infectious laugh, which you could hear right down the other end of the market. She really was a lovely, bubbly person with such a kind heart, but you wouldn't want to mess with her 'cause whilst it was rare to see her lose her temper, if it was aimed at you, you'd be wise to run for the hills.

Stella was there six days a week, brightening up everyone's day with her many funny stories and raucous laugh. Her jewellery was really quite creative and unique and as such her stall was always busy. With the weekends being the busiest, Stella needed help to run her stall on those days so most weekends her daughter, Amy, joined her.

Amy had long auburn hair, usually tied in two plaits which made her look even younger than her twenty-two years. She was very petite with delicate, pretty facial features and large green eyes. Unlike her mum she had a sweet, soft laugh and was also quite shy. Jim was besotted as soon as he set eyes on her.

At the weekends Jim more than ever was excited to get to the market, hoping that Amy would be joining Stella on her stall. He started to pay more attention to his appearance on those days: closer shave, nice clean top and a splash of aftershave. His mum, Rose, winked at his dad and would say, "Our Jim got a girl in tow down the market, Reg," then she'd laugh softly and affectionately ruffle Jim's hair. Reg would wink back and say, "Loads, Rose, they're all over him, he attracts them like a magnet." Jim would just grin; he knew they were only teasing but at the moment, his feelings for Amy he wanted to keep tightly to himself.

To the left of Stella's stall was Ray's, who sold what he liked to call limited edition vinyl records. He always had different music blaring out from various decades, from reggae to classic rock but generally favoured eighties music. Ray was mixed race, being of English and Nigerian heritage, and aside from being very good looking and charming, he was one of the nicest people you could hope to meet.

Jim and Ray got on really well, and would often at the end of the market trading day pop into the market street pub called The Merchant for a couple of pints before heading home. Jim really wanted to try and get Amy to join them at some stage but he didn't want to blow it, so he carried on playing it cool and admiring her from across the crowded market.

Unbeknown to Jim, Amy had indeed noticed him and would covertly watch him when she was sure he couldn't see her doing so. She'd see Jim and Ray head off to the pub; she'd wave goodbye to them and they'd wave back but she never had the guts to ask to join them. Being so shy was a bit of a curse and she so wished she knew how to get his attention. However, Ray had not missed a trick, as he saw them checking each other out then turning away quickly before they got caught. Ray knew how ridiculously shy they both were around each other, but he had a plan.

Ray's girlfriend, Lisa, worked as a stylist in the local hairdressers just around the corner from the market. In fact, they had met when she visited his stall one day, looking for an old Beatles record for her dad. To say it was love at first sight was an understatement, 'cause within weeks they were a steady item and had been relatively inseparable since; that was three years ago.

Ray told Lisa about the situation with Jim and Amy and how he planned to get them together with her help. Lisa often stopped by Stella's stall, chatting to her and Amy and had even bought quite a bit of her jewellery. So the plan she and Ray had come up with was simple enough, which was basically to get Amy to meet her in the pub to help her think about a birthday present she could get Ray for his soon-to-be thirtieth birthday.

The following day being a Saturday, Lisa knew Ray and Jim would be popping to the pub after work, so during her lunch break she headed to Stella's stall, chatted as usual then casually said to Amy, "I need a favour. It's Ray's big three-o next week and I need some ideas on what to get him. Are you free later for a quick drink to help me decide?" Amy hesitated slightly but she got on well with Lisa, so she thought well, why not; it would make a change from just going home and sitting staring at unfunny TV shows with canned laughter. They agreed to meet in the pub at five p.m.

As Amy was leaving to meet Lisa she looked over at Jim, who was busy with a customer, so she just waved bye to Ray and headed off. Ray watched her go, then started packing up his stall and shouted over to Jim, "Ready in five, Jim." Jim gave him the thumbs up and having finished serving his last customer of the day, also began packing up.

Lisa was at the bar when Amy entered and asked her what she wanted to drink. "Half a lager please, Lisa,"; she spotted an empty table and went and sat down. Lisa joined her with their drinks and they both started chatting about Ray's birthday and what Lisa could possibly get him.

The Merchant was a typical market pub, frequented by the market traders and quite a few of the regular market customers. It didn't have a music licence, but the jukebox in the corner was very popular and some nights when the regulars had a few beers the little pub got very lively, with many requests to the landlord, Paul, to turn it up and before long a whole pub sing-song ensued.

Being a Saturday, the pub was already beginning to fill up and there was a tangible feel of excitement in the air, mostly generated by the traders. They had worked long and hard all week and with Sunday being a day off, they planned to have fun this evening and the jukebox was already buzzing. The fruit and veg stall brothers, Tim and Terry, affectionately referred to as The Spuds, were already in high spirits, singing along to the tunes they had each been selecting and greeting everyone they knew with a big pat on the back and an offer to buy them a drink. Yep, their heads were going to be a bit sore come the morning but for now they were enjoying themselves.

Amy was keen to help Lisa decide on a present for Ray, but nearly everything she suggested Lisa turned her nose up at. Amy started to get a sneaky suspicion that Lisa already knew exactly what she was going to get and that she actually had an ulterior motive for inviting her to have a drink. As if on cue the door opened and in walked Ray and Jim. Amy physically gulped and looked at Lisa, who just patted her hand and smiled.

Ray and Jim were immediately captured by The Spuds which thankfully gave Amy time to compose herself. Having spotted Amy as soon as he walked through the door, Jim was also grateful to have been side-lined to shake off the ridiculous nervousness he suddenly felt. What the hell was wrong with him? It was no big deal; he really needed to get a grip.

Amy was also battling with the butterflies that seemed to have started to dance in her belly. Although, she also felt quite excited too; she looked at Lisa, smiled and said, "Do you think Jim likes me?" Lisa burst out laughing and said, "Of course he does, but like you he's also shy, so Ray and I thought you could both do with a little shove." Amy was about to reply but Lisa quickly said, "Shh, they're coming over." Amy's butterflies went into overdrive.

As Ray and Jim appeared at their table, Jim said in a rather strong, confident voice, which he was slightly amazed to hear coming from him, "Hello girls, how you both doing? Can I get you another drink?" Ray quickly said, "It's OK, Jim, I'll get these as it's my round. Girls, what d'you want, same again?" Both Amy and Lisa said in unison, "Yes please," and with that Ray headed to the bar and Jim sat down in the seat next to Amy.

While Ray was at the bar, Lisa was doing most of the talking, mainly about Ray's birthday and how she was arranging a little surprise party here in the pub, which she expected both of them to come along to. Jim listened, nodding where needed while all the time very conscious of the closeness of Amy and the wonderful subtle smell of her perfume, which smelt like crisp, fresh lemons with a hint of sweet peaches. Amy also hardly said a word, but sitting there with Jim sat beside her it felt like something magical was going to happen.

Ray returned from the bar with their drinks and the four of them chatted away, telling each other funny stories about things that had happened while working on the market or at the hairdressers. Before long they were all laughing away like two very happy couples.

Jim got up to get another round of drinks in but Ray said, "Not for me, mate, flipping shattered, need to have a bit of an early one." "Yeah, me too," said Lisa. Amy's heart sank, thinking the night she was so enjoying would be cut short with Jim also deciding to call it a night. However, to her delight Jim looked at her and said, "So, just you and me then, Amy." Amy smiled broadly and nodded in agreement as they both said goodnight to Ray and Lisa, and Jim headed to the bar with the biggest smile ever on his face.

When Jim returned with their drinks, any

awkwardness previously there between them had gone as they talked about their childhoods, their families, places they wanted to visit around the world, favourite food, in fact, all sorts of things as their conversation just seemed to naturally flow. To them it felt like they were the only ones there with just eyes for each other. They were even remarkably oblivious to the line of people dancing, doing the conga over by the jukebox, instigated by The Spuds, and still didn't blink an eyelid as the human conga came dangerously close to their table.

Before they knew it, to their dismay Paul the landlord was shouting, "Time, ladies and gentlemen please, let's be having yer." Jim offered to walk Amy home and as they were leaving, the jukebox was playing its last tune of the night, Roberta Flack, "The First Time Ever I Saw Your Face". Without even thinking, Jim turned to Amy and whispered, "This will always be our song," and kissed her gently on the lips. Yes, the night had definitely been magical for both of them and the start of something so very beautiful.

Jim was brought out of his daydreams by Harry saying, "Jim, popping to the café, you want a cuppa tea?" "Yes please, Harry, that might warm me up a bit."

As Jim felt the warmth of the hot tea between the palms of his hands, he looked over to the stall opposite, which used to be where his good friend Ray had his stall. The stall still sold music but only CDs. The current stallholder, Mike, although selling music, didn't seem to be much of a fan as he never had any music playing. No, not like in Ray's day, when the music would blare out, adding character and vibrancy to the market and putting a smile on everyone's face as they walked by.

Jim felt a twinge of longing for those days when things really did seem just so simple, and of course the great fun he had with Ray while they were working their stalls. Jim again looked up at the sky. Bits of blue were starting to creep through those grey clouds and Jim smiled suddenly, remembering what he was so lucky to have had and what he still very much had.

Jim could still remember that particular day though like it was yesterday, when Ray had indeed acquired a very rare and limited-edition LP. Ray had bought it, like most of his records, from collectors, but this one was sold to him by the family of a man who had sadly passed away, quite young too, being only fifty-six at the time. The man had been a very avid fan of Elvis and had all his albums, which Ray gave the family a good price for. It was one of those hot, sunny days in July and as always Ray was playing his music on the stall, with the day's theme being mostly well-known summer feel-good songs. Ray suddenly let out a yelp of delight whilst frantically beckoning Jim over. Ray showed Jim what he had discovered inside one of the Elvis albums. Jim checked it out, looked back at Ray, whistled slowly then the pair of them threw their arms around each other and were jumping up and down like two overgrown kids, whooping with joy.

Yes, Ray had found his pot of gold because inside one of the albums not only was it signed and dated by Elvis but it also had the original drafting of the songs he had written, with even some unknown songs never recorded. At a Sotheby's auction it went for £4.6 million.

Ray did the right thing and gave a fair percentage to the family who had sold it to him, but there was more than plenty left for him to give Lisa the most wonderful fairy-tale wedding she had been dreaming of, buy a nice house, treat his friends and family and still have enough to not have to worry about money or even working the market six days a week.

What a lucky bugger Ray was, thought Jim, but he so deserved it and it never changed him as he continued being the nicest person ever, whom Jim was proud to have as a friend and whom he still saw on a regular basis.

Jim thought about how rich he was too, not money-wise but being fortunate to have all the riches he could possibly want. He married the love of his life, Amy, who gave him two beautiful daughters, Lily and Daisy, who were both the spitting image of their mum, but taller, which no doubt came from him. He was also so very lucky to still have his mum and dad around, Rose and Reg, who totally doted on their grandchildren. Yes, life had been very kind to him. Amy sadly had lost her mum, Stella, a couple of years back but echoes of her wonderful laugh could be heard in the laughter of his two daughters.

Jim looked around him. This market had been such a big part of his life where he had grown from boy to man, met good friends, fell in love and made a good honest living surrounded by the most warm-hearted, genuine and hardworking people.

The blue sky was now winning against the grey clouds; the market was beginning to see the first customers of the day slowly milling around. The market had been the beating heart of this community for generations and whilst not as busy as it used to be, still people came for the bargains but more importantly to be part of something real, alive and exciting.

Jim smiled, thinking just how lucky he was and even though there would always be some gloomy, wet days, he wouldn't change his market life for anything and most definitely not to work in what he considered to be a soulless supermarket.

TWO MINDS, ONE HEAD

Helen had always been indecisive from as far back as she could remember; in fact, she was well known for frequently saying, "Umm, I'm in two minds about that." She knew it drove her family and friends crazy, with some of her less understanding friends, Jane in particular, often getting frustrated with her and almost shouting at her, "Helen, please just make a decision, it's not that difficult." It was for her.

She had a vivid memory of when she was about eight years old, being in a department store with her mum to look for a dress for her for a family wedding. She could still see her mum now, holding up a handful of equally pretty dresses and saying in quite an exasperated voice, "Helen, we've been here almost an hour; if you don't choose, I'll pick one for you." Helen had looked from her mum to the dresses and said, "Well, I like the pink one but I'm also in two minds about the yellow and blue one." With that her mum took her by the hand, marched over to the checkout and told the cashier, "We'll take the pink one, thank you." Helen was about to say that actually the yellow one might be better, but the stern look on her mum's face, which seemed to silently say, "You dare," stopped her before any words escaped her lips.

As she got older her indecisiveness seemed to become more intense, where simple things like walking into a coffee shop and ordering a coffee to go seemed to take ages; you certainly wouldn't want to be behind her in a queue. Yes, her "two minds" syndrome, together with her newly acquired lack of confidence where she started to doubt her own abilities, was turning into a bit of a nightmare, not just for Helen but for everyone around her. However, it also sometimes worked to her advantage as some people, particularly men, found it endearing and during one of her indecisive moments, that's when she met Geoff.

Geoff was twenty-six, not your typical tall, dark and handsome at five feet 8 inches and stockily built, but with his glossy black shoulder-length hair, which girls wanted to run their fingers through, blue eyes and dazzling smile with a perfect set of white teeth, he was definitely eye-catching. Although, he was very unaware of his own attractiveness and seemed oblivious to the admiring glances from women in the office or when walking down the street.

Geoff worked in an advertising agency as a copywriter, although having only worked there for six months he was yet to establish himself and seemed to spend a large part of the day running to get coffee for the account director and her executive team. Geoff was very good at what he did and he was keen to show off his copywriting skills, but as yet the right opportunity had not arisen. He knew it was only a matter of time and for now he would just smile and be the coffee shop runner.

It was a warm, sunny day in July and as Geoff walked out of the advertising building and crossed the road to the coffee shop, he noticed there was quite a queue, which was rather unusual for this time of the day. Geoff took his place at the back of the line. The man in front of him, wearing a very formal navy pinstripe three-piece suit was mumbling under his breath, "Come on, hurry up and make a decision." Geoff looked to the front of the queue, where there was a girl who looked about twenty-four with long blonde hair, wearing a fairly short, pink flowery summer dress which from behind showed off her very shapely tanned legs.

The girl was looking up at the extensive coffee menu on the wall but was clearly struggling with what to have. The barista was looking inpatient and Geoff noted a few more people waiting, tutting and grumbling. Without a thought Geoff headed to the front, stood beside the girl and said, "I come here a lot so maybe I can help you decide; personally, I'd recommend the double cream cappuccino with sprinkled chocolate." The girl looked at him and then for the first time saw the queue and the unhappy faces, and quickly nodded in agreement. Before she could change her mind Geoff took charge and said, "Two of those to go, please." Geoff paid for the drinks, gently took her elbow and led her out, passing a line of very relieved customers, mister navy pinstripe in particular.

Geoff would need to go back in as he had a large coffee order for the office, but for now he led the girl over to the outside seating area and indicated with his hand for her to sit down as he handed her the coffee. She gratefully accepted, smiled and said, "Thank you, that was really kind of you. My name is Helen, by the way." Geoff introduced himself and they chatted for a few moments, until Geoff explained that he needed to get back to the office but maybe they could meet up again, which Helen happily agreed to and they arranged to do so the following day.

Helen and Geoff met at the same coffee shop the next day and continued to for a few weeks, as this became their meeting place. They had quite a lot in common, having similar backgrounds: both had achieved a first English degree, albeit from different universities, and they both had a passion for creative writing. Helen told Geoff about her job as a PA to the assistant editor of a large local newspaper company; her aim was to eventually become a columnist. Geoff shared his goal of becoming a renowned copywriter within the field of advertising.

It wasn't long, before their coffee catch ups turned to meeting for dinner, although Geoff soon learned not to leave it up to Helen to choose the venue or they'd never get anywhere. He tended to always make the restaurant reservations and then let Helen know where they were going to meet.

They had only been seeing each other for a couple of months but Geoff was really starting to fall for Helen, and found himself daydreaming about her throughout the day and couldn't wait to see her. He thought about her dark brown eyes and how they would blink rapidly when she was having trouble making a decision, which was often;

her tiny, cute button nose and her delicate, small hands, which he found himself reaching for more and more whenever they were together. He knew she liked him but he wasn't sure just how much as she had not really shown any strong feelings towards him. Unbeknown to him, Helen had been going over and over in her head about how she felt about Geoff and had finally come to a decision, and was going to tell him when they met that night.

Geoff had chosen a lovely little French bistro just round the corner from both their offices and the table was booked for seven p.m. Geoff had bought a change of clothes into the office as he was lucky enough to have the use of staff shower facilities. Helen had left work dead on five and rushed home to get ready for her evening with Geoff; thinking about what she needed to say to him made her feel rather nervous.

Once home Helen tried to focus on what to wear, which as always was a challenge. While she had whittled it down to three potential outfits, she was in two minds which one would be best for this evening and the conversation she knew she needed to have with Geoff. She looked at her watch: it was almost six thirty and she hadn't even showered yet, but thankfully she had washed her hair that morning.

Helen's eyes were blinking like crazy. She looked in the mirror and said out loud, "What is wrong with me, why can't I just easily make a decision?" She had a very quick shower, then not wanting to be too late, she closed her eyes, randomly picked up one of the outfits and quickly put it on, did her make-up, brushed her long blonde hair, slipped into the shoes that went with the outfit, choice thankfully taken out of her hands, grabbed her keys and bag and with one last look in the mirror, headed for the door. It was now just gone seven but amazingly a black cab flashing its free yellow sign was coming down the road. She hailed it, jumped in, gave the driver the address of the restaurant and sat back with her thoughts on the evening ahead and how Geoff would react to what she planned to tell him.

Geoff had chosen a casual but smart look for this evening, with a pair of dark jeans and a long-sleeved white button-down shirt with subtle blue edging around the collar and wrists. He had arrived ten minutes early at the restaurant, was shown to his table and waited for Helen. For some reason he felt slightly nervous, which was odd as all the times he had previously met Helen he hadn't felt that way, but his senses were telling him that something was going to happen tonight which made him feel worried and also excited at the same time.

Geoff looked at his watch, which said 7.13 p.m., and as he looked up, there stood Helen in the doorway. She looked absolutely breathtaking in a black lacy dress which came to the knee, again showing off her wonderful legs, with quarter-length sleeves and a heart-shaped neckline. Around her neck she wore a silver diamanté choker with matching earrings; the handbag she carried was also black with a tiny diamanté clasp which matched her shoes. As she walked towards the table she smiled. Geoff got up to greet her and kissed her on the cheek as he held out her chair for her to sit down.

For a moment they both just stared at each other, lost

in their own thoughts. Geoff was looking at Helen and thinking he had never seen her looking more lovely, and Helen was thinking how gorgeous he looked and also what she knew she had to tell him this evening.

The waiter came to take their drinks order and Geoff suggested a bottle of Sauvignon Blanc, which he knew Helen liked: she just nodded in agreement. The waiter asked if they knew what they wanted to eat, or did they need a moment? Geoff smiled, as from experience he knew they'd need more than a moment, as they could be well on their way to a second bottle before Helen made a decision on what she wanted to eat. However, to his surprise, without him even noticing her looking at the menu, Helen looked at the waiter and said, "I'll have the French onion soup as a main, please." Geoff was speechless for a few seconds but then quickly asked for the same.

The waiter poured their wine and left the bottle in a cooler at the side of the table. Helen and Geoff made small talk which was unusual as their conversations were normally quite animated and not at all strained. They both seemed to welcome the interruption by the waiter bringing their food as the tension building between them was becoming tangible.

They silently looked at their large bowls of soup and attempted to eat, but as good as it looked, they both seemed to have lost their appetite and were just pushing the contents round the bowl. Geoff suddenly reached over and took Helen's hand that was resting on the table. She didn't pull her hand away but she also didn't clutch his hand either. Geoff couldn't bear it any longer and said,

"What's the matter, Helen, is something bothering you? You seem very distant tonight." Helen sighed deeply, pushed her bowl away, took a sip of wine and thought, OK, it's now or never.

Helen looked over at Geoff, who was eagerly waiting for her to say something. She took a deep breath and then blurted out, "Geoff, I really like you." Geoff held his breath as he could hear a "but" coming. "But…" There it was, thought Geoff, and his heart sank. "But I feel like I'm really getting to like you too much, which is worrying because I know I can be so frustrating when I take so long at choosing something and soon this will annoy you and I just couldn't bear to see your frustration with me in your eyes. Therefore, I really need you to be honest with me and let me know now if my indecisiveness is something that you could not deal with long-term before I get in too deep."

Geoff just stared at her in disbelief and it was now Helen's turn to anxiously wait for him to speak. Geoff looked at this beautiful person sitting opposite him who had just shown him her vulnerability, and his feelings for her at that moment had intensified; he just wanted to wrap her in his arms and never let her go. Instead, he took both of her hands in his, looked into her beautiful brown eyes and said, "Helen, being unable to make quick decisions is just part of who you are but that could never detract from the warm, generous, funny, intelligent and passionate person you are and the person I have come to adore over the last few months." Geoff did then stand up and pull her into his arms and kiss her long and hard, right there in front of all the other diners and staff who all rewarded them, when they came up for air, with a round of spontaneous applause. Helen and Geoff left soon after, two very happy people, and headed to Geoff's flat where they continued what they'd started at the restaurant in private, and we're not talking about the soup.

That was just over a year ago and here Helen now stood at the train station, staring up at the many destinations, struggling to choose where to go. She thought of the events of the night before and was just so embarrassed she just had to get away; but where? Her two minds were at it again.

She got up early that morning and rang her boss to say she needed to take a couple of days off. She was definitely well overdue some leave as she had been working non-stop for the past few weeks so her boss, Derek, readily agreed. She packed a few overnight things and headed for the station. As she continued to stare at the many destinations, her mind, or two minds, kept pulling her back to the previous evening and the look of horror on Geoff's face. Whatever had possessed her? She should have known better.

Geoff had been frantically trying to get hold of her since she ran out of the restaurant the night before but her phone just kept going to voicemail. He had tried to run after her but his access was blocked by a few customers entering the restaurant, and when he got onto the street she was nowhere to be seen. No doubt she was in the taxi he could see just turning the corner at the top of the road.

Geoff kept thinking about what had happened and having come to know Helen so well, he knew she would have misread his reaction and then just wanted to get herself as far away from him as she possibly could. He needed to find her though to put things right, but where could she be?

Geoff called her office and was informed that she had taken a couple of days' leave but they didn't know where she intended to go. To be honest, Helen probably hadn't made her mind up yet, thought Geoff. He suddenly remembered a conversation they'd had quite recently about travelling; he thought he knew where she might be and made his way there, hoping he was right.

Geoff and Helen had recently talked about where would be their first port of call when they ever had that feeling of running for the hills. Geoff recalled how they playfully disagreed with each other, both believing their option was best. They had really teased each other but ended up laughing, with Helen conceding that in her case, it would hardly be "running" as it would no doubt take days for her to make a decision on where to run to. Geoff smiled at the memory and just hoped he was in time before she had indeed headed for the hills.

Helen still stood staring at the board but not really looking as she was thinking about what had happened. Helen had planned everything so carefully, booking their favourite little French bistro, liaising with the restaurant staff on her plan and swearing them to secrecy. How could she have got it so wrong though, as she really believed this was what Geoff also wanted. She put her head in her hands as the moment in question flashed across her mind.

She'd set the scene by arranging with the restaurant for Geoff to be served a special double cream cappuccino with chocolate sprinkled on the top, but also something extra added on the cream. The waiter had served the coffee and stood back with an anticipatory smile on his face. As Geoff looked at the special coffee, which of course was significant to when they had first met, he looked over at Helen, who first told him to look closer at the contents of his coffee. Geoff noticed the ring and then as if in slow motion he heard Helen say, "I love you, Geoff, will you marry me?" His face must have portrayed something very different from what he was feeling because before he knew what was happening, Helen was running out of the restaurant.

Geoff arrived at the station and started looking around for Helen. Then he saw her staring up at the destinations board. He watched her for a moment, his heart going out to her as he knew she'd be beating herself up about how a night he knew she would have spent so much time deciding on how to make special had not gone to plan, and it was all his fault.

He approached her slowly, then standing beside her said, "I come here a lot so maybe I can help you decide." She turned to face him and burst into tears. Geoff took her hand in his while wiping her tears away with a tissue he found in his pocket. Geoff explained that he realised that to her, his initial expression last night may have looked like horror at what she had proposed, but that couldn't have been further from the truth. It was actually shock at hearing that such a beautiful person like Helen wanted to spend the rest of her life with him.

Helen smiled weakly as Geoff took her in his arms and said, "Helen, it would be the greatest honour to become your husband, but I must insist on choosing our honeymoon destination as you will always be in two minds about where we should go." Helen then cried tears of joy as they both linked arms and headed off home to make plans for their new life together.

PARENT BASH

Now, I have this terrible dream: two burly men hurting my eighty-year-old mum, which is upsetting beyond belief. But in the dream, I shout, "Leave her alone, it's not your job to hurt her, its mine." Well, of course we don't ever want to hurt our parents, but we so do daily sometimes!

The hurt we cause is, mostly, unintentional because I'm sure if we knew what effect our actions were having on our parents, we surely wouldn't do what we sometimes do oh, so very casually.

So, what does this unintentional hurt look like? Well, we start at an early age, sadly, like shrugging our parents off when they try to give us a cuddle at the school gate. We didn't think we were hurting our parents as we just felt embarrassed in front of the other kids, who in turn were also pushing away their own parents! So, there it is, that tiny stab at the parent's heart.

Then the terrible teenager years when I'm sure everyone, after turning thirteen, has at some time shouted hysterically at their mum or dad, "I hate you!" Wow, that really is a full-blown punch in the heart.

Then the late teens when the arrogance kicks in and the child deludedly believes they invented everything, knows all there is to know and their parents know nothing.

Then staying out late or even all night, without a word to the parents or a thought of the worry and anguish being caused to the poor parent pacing the floors, looking out the window in search of their young adult child with terrible thoughts going through their head of what might have happened to them.

No, the child is oblivious to the pain they are causing as they're too busy having a good time, with absolutely no understanding as to why their parents would be fretting.

The child is then older and the parents become grandparents, completely doting on their grandchildren. Although, the child still manages to unknowingly hurt their parents by not recognising just how much the parents were looking forward to the planned family get-together, which the child just so casually cancels at the last minute.

I think when you have children of your own, its only then that you realise the hurt, pain and anguish you inflicted on your mum and dad. Maybe payback!

Parents tend to hide the pain they feel from their offspring because they don't want to hurt them by letting them know how their actions have hurt them!

It's all so sad: why are we all too proud and less honest about how we feel? You know, if we were less proud and more honest, it could save a lot of heartache.

Then there's the pain the parent unknowingly causes the child, but that's another story!

DYING: WHAT THE HELL?
LIVING: FIND THE HEAVEN!

Well, whilst I know I'm in no way unique in experiencing the loss of a loved one, I'm definitely not a stranger to it. In fact, it's become quite a habit, whereby I swear the police will soon be asking me for an alibi!

The pain felt is a physical thing though, like you've been beaten up by five professional heavyweight boxers, or repeatedly run over by a double decker bus. The world as you knew it has gone; you start to function on a different level, like you're in a vacuum, being dragged further and further down into a pit of dark despair. You feel strangely removed from everything continuing to carry on around you, but your hurt and anguish is on parade like a flashing neon sign in your face, highlighting your lightless dull eyes for all to see so clearly.

It's amazing though, as even when we are in the throes of such immense sadness, a funny or lighter moment breaks its way through and like on autopilot, we laugh. It's not laughter that comes from happiness though, more like a spontaneous burst of emotion, but nevertheless for that tiny minuscule moment in time, the light in your eyes flickers and whilst full beam is not restored, there's that first appearance of hope.

So, what's it all about? Well, we know we're born, we live, we die, unless you believe yourself to be immortal of course. The life we are born into is not a "one size fits all", nor is dying and grief: it is most definitely a very personal thing.

The loss of someone you have loved so very deeply is not something you ever "get over", as some people who have yet to actually experience it so casually tell those who have, "Oh, hang in there, you'll get over this!" No, you seriously don't; you just learn to live with it.

Grieving comes in all shapes and sizes with many different coping mechanisms. I was raised as a Catholic and whilst no longer a practicing Catholic, I still have a strong sense of faith in whatever lays beyond. Really, I feel there is so much more and believing in an afterlife helped me get through those oh, so very dark depths-of-despair days.

Some people act completely out of character, go off the rails a bit, throw caution to the wind, live dangerously and seek solace in alcohol, drugs, food, or even loveless sex. Where someone has lost their life partner, some people enter into another relationship far too quickly believing that will help, but most of the time it doesn't; it just makes them feel more bereft, lonely and then they beat themselves up with feelings of guilt and betrayal.

My first feeling of loss was when my grandad died and then my nan and, on both occasions, I can remember exactly where I was when I was told the news and how I reacted. I cried my eyes out of course and remember thinking how could this happen? They were really good people; it was so unfair. Later experiences were beloved aunts and uncles, where once again I cried and felt so terribly sad. However, the first time I met the real deal grief was when my dad died suddenly: now that was my first introduction to such raw, off-the-scale emotions.

You see, while you may have already lost other people you cared for, losing a parent is like the first smack-in-the face realisation that dying is what is waiting around that corner for all of us. Which corner we do not know, but it's there.

I can still remember that feeling of utter shock and devastation when my dad died, and there were a couple of songs at that time that I couldn't bear to hear: "The Living Years" by Mike and The Mechanics, especially the lyric, "I wasn't there that morning when my father passed away, I didn't get to tell him all the things I had to say." Also, *Dance with my Father* by Luther Vandross was just too sad to bear.

It's funny the things that stick in your brain though, just after someone has died. After my dad died, I always remember seeing his slippers by his chair, just like they were waiting for him to slip his feet into them and ease back into his chair, like I'd seen him do so many times. Or his little King Charles dog sitting by the door, waiting for him to walk through it.

It's been twenty-four years now and whilst the pain is no longer with me and I'm able to think of my dad and smile, I still miss him so very much and still struggle to listen to those particular songs.

Grieving is a process of many stages but there is no set pattern or time frame as again, it's an individual thing. So, in no order we have shock, disbelief, denial, pain, sadness, depression, anger and acceptance.

So, are there different types of grief itself? Yes, I believe there are; not that the pain is any less, but its magnitude can be.

Now, losing my dad was, as said, my first introduction to the reality of "death as we know it". I would never have believed that the raw, sad emotions felt at that time could ever be worse. Oh, how I was wrong as when my husband died, the five boxers became twenty and the double decker bus turned into ten steam trains.

Basically, my world exploded and while I knew I was still alive, as I was breathing, I didn't feel or even want to be part of the living. Initially, shock and denial kicked in, closely followed by me howling like a wounded animal, actions which I had absolutely no control over. I felt like my body had been taken over by demons, and in the eyes of my childhood priests and nuns, I was probably a likely candidate for a good old exorcism.

Other people's behaviour was interesting, like crossing the road to avoid me as they just didn't know what to say to me. I understood, I didn't blame them; I mean, what could they say, "Sorry, why, it's not your fault." Although, the ones who said within months, "Are you dating yet?", well, to them I would have liked to have said, "No, have you found your brain yet!" But I didn't, of course, I just looked at them like they were a totally alien species, devoid of any emotion.

Sadness and deep depression soon arrived, where I felt hollow inside; completely empty. I saw no point in anything, but I had two children who needed me then more than ever, so they were my strength and my focus.

So, I kept punching.

Now, I use the word "punching" as a metaphor and not as a physical action. It was a term my husband used as words of encouragement whenever someone was having a bad time. "Keep punching" he'd say, with that wonderful smile of his.

No, going around punching people's lights out was not what I did. However, the stage of anger hit me big time, where I'd have these moments of pure uncontrollable anger that would appear out of nowhere: my "red mist over the eyes" days. I tended to unleash my anger at work situations, whereby if the slightest little thing at work went wrong or didn't go my way, I would blow. My work colleagues and managers were understanding, and I was always so remorseful after my latest episode of my eyes flashing, stomping about the office, arguing with people, and basically behaving in such an unprofessional manner. Although, whilst I couldn't seem to control these outbursts, I knew they had to stop.

My pain and sadness were with me every day but my dark days started to get further and further apart, as thankfully did my red mist days.

I started to read a lot of books about spiritualism and other people's experiences of how they coped with their loss. Spirituality gave me faith and hope and hearing about other people's stories made me feel I was not alone in my suffering.

I also considered myself lucky as I had such great support around me from family and really good friends; some people weren't so lucky. So, I started to learn to live a different life and the healing began.

This Valentine's Day, it will be eleven years since I lost the love of my life, the irony of it being the day of love does not go unnoticed! I miss him still every day and know I always will, as he was so very unique, beautiful inside and out and for me no one could ever steal his thunder.

Now the grief of losing our beloved pets, again no less painful as they are of course part of our family. Although, do we accept this loss more easily, being conditioned from when we are very young to their inevitably short lifespan? Well, maybe this notion depends on individual circumstances because if a dog, cat, budgie or rabbit are all we have then they are our world, with the loss no doubt unbearable.

With the knowledge of knowing our pets are more than likely going to pop their furry clogs before we do, maybe this was how I started to feel about my mum, who was in her eighties and not in good health. I think, looking back, I was subconsciously preparing myself for what I knew was on the horizon.

The call I had been so fearful of and dreading finally came. I am thankful though that I was able to get there in time and as she passed away peacefully, I held her in my arms, stroking her hair and singing her favourite songs. So, now I am an orphan.

Your mum is truly the one who loves you so unconditionally and there will never be anyone one hundred per cent always totally on your side. The loss of my lovely mum is tremendous but as strange as it sounds, I feel I was more prepared this time.

For my own personal grief, some of the hardest moments have been going to work or meeting up with friends and family with a smile on my face, joking and laughing while inside my heart is weeping. But it's my grief, not theirs, so why should they have to endure my pain? I don't want that to sound like I'm some kind if martyr; I'm not, I just didn't want people to think of me as a negative person, a human lemon, where little by little they'd start to make excuses about meeting up or even worse, just pity me.

Nothing is certain in life except knowing that dying is inevitable. Life itself is a precious journey, not to be taken for granted, so don't waste another day, grab it by the throat and laugh, dance and sing and most importantly, keep punching!

DEADLY SWEET!

Mulberry was a very pretty market town with the river Mul running through the middle. Black and white Elizabethan-style town houses all sat side by side along the cobblestone High Street, with many little independent shops selling wonderful unique items, such as luxury soaps in many different creative designs and birthstone gifts made out of blown glass in all various colours and sizes.

There were a number of bridges across the river, some made of stone and some made of wood, with one very spectacular metal bridge with heart-shaped pillars on each side that was lit up at night by many twinkling lights encased around the metal hearts.

There were a variety of restaurants and bars along each side of the river, serving food to meet everyone's taste buds, from Italian to a selection of vegetarian dishes. During the summer months you'd be wise to book well in advance if you wanted to enjoy al fresco dining in such a lovely location, whilst taking in the view of the river and its activities such as canoeing and paddle boating, the church peeking over the houses, which seemed to watch over the town and its inhabitants like a protector and the luscious green hills beyond, reaching high into the sky.

The town also had three independent tea shops, all serving traditional afternoon tea with a selection of crust-free sandwiches, scones, jams and miniature fancy cakes. All the tea shops were popular with both residents and visitors alike but the competition between the owners was taken very seriously, with them all thriving to be the best little tea shop in town. The competition was friendly enough but one of the owners was planning on stopping at nothing to make sure her shop stood out from the rest. Aside from her intentions not being honest, a very dark side of her was about to be unleashed on the other unsuspecting tea shop owners, and their customers too.

Teacosy was in a very good location at the beginning of the High St, capturing those visitors first arriving into Mulberry already fancying a nice cuppa and slice of cake before exploring the town. The owner, Marjorie, was a lovely, happy person who always welcomed everyone who walked through the door with a beaming smile, whilst highlighting the delightful home-made cakes available that day.

Marjorie had owned Teacosy for almost twenty-five years when she and her husband, Charlie, had moved to the town after taking early retirement from quite stressful jobs working in Children's Social Services in London. They sold their flat in London, bought a nice little terrace house in Mulberry and put the rest of their money into Teacosy. Charlie did help out at the tea shop but it really was Marjorie's pride and joy, and she worked so hard to make sure people kept coming along to enjoy her homemade delights and also the warm welcome they always received.

Purple Teapot could be found in the middle of the High Street, next to a tourist shop selling postcards, tea towels, fridge magnets and small framed photos of Mulberry and was managed by Ken, who was well into his seventies. Ken was very friendly but also way too talkative, so anyone popping in the shop usually needed to be revived with a nice pot of tea in the Purple Teapot next door.

Mary was in her early forties, had lived in Mulberry all her life and had worked in the Purple Teapot for just over ten years, since she was made redundant from the bus company's head office where she had worked as an administrative assistant. Unfortunately, following the discontinuation of some of the bus routes, her workload ceased and she was no longer required.

Mary was not the happiest of people and smiling did not come naturally to her, but she did love her job and tried really hard to offer good customer service and make people feel welcome. The owner, Cecil, was very hands-off and Mary only really saw him at the end of the day when he collected the day's takings. He didn't really have much interest in the tea shop itself, just the money it made, but he was always appreciative of Mary and recognised that she was a good little worker, so mainly let her get on with it. This totally suited Mary as this arrangement made her feel like the Purple Teapot actually belonged to her, and customers even just assumed that she was the owner.

At the end of the High Street, just on the bend with a lovely view of the river, was Strawberry Jam, owned and run by a rather formidable lady called Angela. Strawberry

Jam was previously a sweet shop and when Angela bought the premises fifteen years earlier, she totally renovated it and created a modern, shabby chic look which was both charming and indulgent, with subtle pastel colours of pale green and yellow giving it a cosy and relaxing feel.

Angela was in her early fifties and her life had not been a bed of roses. She got pregnant at sixteen by a boy in her class at school and whose parents were even more horrified than her own. Despite many arguments against from both sets of parents, Angela decided to have the baby, which was born seven months later, prematurely weighing only four pounds. After a few weeks in the hospital the baby girl was allowed home to live with Angela and her parents. Angela called her Isabelle and seriously thought her heart would burst with the love she felt for the tiny baby she held in her arms.

A few years later Angela met and married a man she thought was perfect, although sadly turned out to be anything but. He controlled and manipulated her to the extent that his actions seriously affected her overall well-being, but with the help of her parents and friends she got the strength to leave him, subsequently divorced him and decided a change of scene was definitely needed. Having done quite a bit of research she eventually came across the market town of Mulberry, which seemed ideal.

The three tea shop ladies, whilst not strictly friends were always very pleasant to each other when they met at local functions or when going about their usual business in the town, such as going to the supermarket or bank. Their conversations usually revolved around their respective tea shops or issues involving the town in general, but they never discussed any personal details about themselves so what they knew about the other was either speculation or what they'd heard from other town residents.

Colin and Jake, both in their late forties, had moved to Mulberry almost nine years ago, just after tying the knot in what was then called a civil partnership. They had both previously lived in a large town in Buckinghamshire where they met at a mutual friend's wedding and where from that day were pretty much inseparable.

Both Colin and Jake had very creative minds and enjoyed creating beautiful outdoor garden spaces with many different plants and flowers. They were both looking for a new venture away from such a large town and what they considered to be rather mundane jobs: they both worked in the insurance industry, albeit different companies. So, when one of Jake's colleagues happened to mention, just in passing really, that his uncle was looking for someone to manage his flower shop in a quaint market town, Jake was all ears. As soon as he got home, Jake excitedly talked about it with Colin, who was equally excited and so the next day Jake arranged to meet the uncle and subsequently within a matter of months Jake and Colin had quit their jobs, given notice on their rented apartment and were off to start a new life in Mulberry.

Colin and Jake were two of the most generous and kind people you could meet and always keen to support other businesses in the town. In particular they regularly bought items from the local shops and also frequently visited the three tea shops, being mindful of not showing favouritism to any of the tea shops as they knew each owner was vying to be the best and that each owner was also quite possessive over their regular customers. Colin and Jake most certainly didn't want to offend any one of them, so they spread their visiting time evenly across all three, which they felt all the owners would be fine with. However, one of the owners was most definitely not fine with this as she saw it as a betrayal which they would pay for when the plan she was hatching came together.

The flower shop was everything Colin and Jake had hoped for and with their hard work and artistic touches, they turned the once rather tired little shop into a vibrant and colourful place with an ever changing, eye-catching window display enticing people inside. Yes, they had really brightened up the far end of the High Street where the flower shop was situated and had definitely increased profits for the owner, who in turn paid them a very good salary as his little shop had never seen such good business.

It was approaching Valentine's Day and Jake was in the shop window, creating a wonderful heart display from red roses and pink carnations. Across the road the teashop owner watched him and while she had to agree how beautiful the window display looked, she was thinking of her plan to ruin the other two tea shops and how Colin and Jake were unwittingly going to be part of it.

Most mornings in the flower shop were pretty busy, so by about two p.m. they would shut the shop for an hour and head to one of the tea shops next on their list to visit. As they sat in the tea shop enjoying their tea and cake, the owner chatted with them in between serving other customers and was very complimentary about their window display, which really pleased Colin and Jake, who as lovely as they both were, really couldn't get enough flattery.

As they were getting up to leave the owner said, "Now, boys, you know how much I appreciate your regular custom but don't think I don't know about you also frequenting both the other tea shops." They both stared at her wide-eyed, like two naughty school boys caught with their hands in the cookie jar, but before they could say anything she just laughed and said, "Don't look so worried, I haven't got a problem with that. I think it's great how you want to support us and keep all three of us happy." The relief on Colin and Jake's faces was really quite comical. She then asked them a favour which she needed them to agree to for her plan to work.

The teashop owner told them how she was looking at introducing homemade toffee sweets to her menu but first of all wanted to see if people would like them, so she was hoping they would help her with some covert tasting. She managed to persuade them to take a supply she had recently made to both the other tea shops, pretending they had made them but before they considered selling them in the flower shop as a side line, they would want to know if people liked them so would be grateful if these could be given out as complimentary sweets to the tea shop customers and at the same time request feedback on the taste.

As always Colin and Jake were happy to help and with them both being so thoughtful and nice, they were not suspicious at all about the tea shop owner's real motive. So, the next day when visiting the next planned tea shop, they did exactly what they had been asked and the following day they repeated the plan in the remaining tea shop. Both tea shops were more than happy to help the boys out and promised to update them on their customers' feedback as soon as possible.

A couple of days later, Jake was working on his new window display and Colin had just finished selling a beautiful mixed bouquet of freesias, white carnations and yellow roses to a customer for his mother's birthday. Suddenly there was a piercing wailing from an emergency services siren, which was quite an infrequent sound to hear in Mulberry. Colin and Jake headed out into the street to see what was going on.

Just a little bit up the High Street from their shop they saw an ambulance pull up outside the Purple Teapot. Cecil, whom the boys believed to be Mary the owner's silent business partner, looked very worried, and greeted the paramedics. Ken, from the shop next door, had also appeared and stood next to Cecil. The paramedics and Cecil headed inside the tea shop and Ken, looking up and down the street, noticed Colin and Jake and made a beeline for them.

As Ken approached, Colin said, "Whatever has happened?" Ken, almost talking ten to the dozen, blurted out that apparently a couple of customers had become violently sick after eating in the Purple Teapot, throwing up everywhere by all accounts, so Mary had called an ambulance and then Cecil. "Oh no, that's terrible, but they must have been allergic to something; it couldn't be food poisoning as Mary kept the place spotless," said Jake. The three of them continued to watch as the paramedics, one by one, took two people out on stretchers, placed them carefully in the ambulance and then off it went with its siren wailing and blue lights flashing.

After about ten minutes, Colin and Jake were able to excuse themselves from Ken, who really hadn't stopped talking for the whole time, and head back into their shop. They both really hoped Mary was OK and agreed to check in on her later.

As they were closing up for the day there was another wailing siren heading down the High Street, which went past them and pulled to a halt outside Strawberry Jam. Colin and Jake looked at each other and both said in unison, "What is going on here?"

Colin and Jake were beyond curious now, as two ambulances in one day here in Mulberry was unheard of. They walked towards the tea shop to see if they could help in any way and before they knew it, Ken was also walking with them. Angela, the owner, was outside talking to the paramedics and they could hear her say that a family of three, out of nowhere, had all started vomiting and holding their stomachs in agony. The paramedics and Angela then went back inside and within a few moments another ambulance had arrived, and the family were each being helped into the ambulances which then took off, heading for the hospital. Angela, Colin and Jake looked stunned and Ken for once was unnaturally silent.

Marjorie heard the sirens and innocently said to her customers, "Oh, I wonder what all the commotion is," as she secretly smiled, knowing that her plan had very likely succeeded.

The unusual events of the day very quickly spread through the town, with everyone talking about them and wondering what on earth had occurred. It didn't take long though for everyone to find out what actually had happened, as by the next day tests taken at the hospital determined that all the customers from both tea shops had been poisoned and the evidence seemed to suggest that the poison had been placed inside some homemade toffee sweets! Luckily, following rapid treatment from the hospital clinicians, all the customers were now slowly recovering, but of course they all wanted answers so the incident was now in the hands of the police.

Colin and Jake, on hearing the news, were totally shocked but also very worried as they were the ones who had shared the sweets with the tea shops. They knew they had to go to the police station and tell them what had happened but as they were about to leave, two police officers appeared in the flower shop asked them to confirm who they were, then arrested them on suspicion of poisoning with intent to harm.

News about the boys' arrest had filtered through to Marjorie and whilst slightly concerned, it was going to be their word against hers and she felt confident that the police would believe her, as she could be very convincing. In fact, she thought she should have been an actress and gave out a little chuckle, which was louder than she thought as a few of her customers stopped their chatting and looked over at her.

Marjorie's resentment of the other two tea shops and

their owners had started a few years back, when it was clear to her that despite her best efforts, customers seemed to prefer to go to the Purple Teapot or Strawberry Jam. Well, she wasn't having it; she'd been here a lot longer than them and she wasn't going to let them win. Marjorie hadn't started off with the plan of poisoning the customers who visited the other tea shops and framing the boys for it; no, she just wanted all the customers to come to her instead. Every time she saw customers looking in her window then heard them say, "Let's go to one of the other tea shops further on as they're much nicer," her resentment turned to anger, where her state of mind was becoming very unstable.

At the police station Colin and Jake were questioned under caution separately. Both were equally distraught but their stories matched and without any current evidence they were released but warned that they were still suspects, so they were not to leave town and were to be available for further questioning.

The two detectives investigating the case reviewed the boys' statements and then headed to Teacosy to question the owner about the claims that had been made against her.

Marjorie was alone in the shop with no customers when the detectives walked in and introduced themselves. She had been expecting them and had been rehearsing what to say. Marjorie put on her biggest sweetest smile, which the detectives thought actually looked quite menacing, and offered them something to drink and one of her homemade cakes, which they both politely declined. They asked her about the sweets and informed her of Colin and Jake's claim that she had made them and asked them to carry out some covert tasting by sharing with the other tea shops to give to their customers as complimentary and then obtain their feedback.

Marjorie continued to smile what she believed to be sweetly, but this is not what the detectives saw as to them she was sneering, and her eyes looked quite wild. She told them that she had never made any kind of sweets as her speciality was cakes, and the only reason she could think of that the boys were trying to point the finger at her was because she unfortunately had to stop them coming into her tea shop, as they were always rude and sometimes even abusive to her customers. The detectives just nodded and made notes and then asked if she would mind if they had a quick look in her kitchen. Marjorie wasn't concerned as she had covered her tracks, so she stood up and showed them the way.

The kitchen was absolutely spotless and as they looked around, aside from a very strong smell of bleach, there didn't appear to be anything untoward. Marjorie continued to smile at the detectives, which was beginning to look more and more sinister, to the point where they were convinced something was not quite right.

Marjorie had indeed done a very good job of cleaning the bowls and utensils she had used to make the poisoned toffee sweets, and whilst the rat poison was still there under the sink, this was not an unusual item to have in a domestic kitchen. Yes, Marjorie was feeling very pleased with herself and was getting ready to show the detectives out. The detectives were indeed about to leave when one of them noticed something just poking out from under one of the cabinets next to the oven. As he walked over towards the object, Marjorie followed his gaze and instantly saw what was there. As he bent down to pick it up, Marjorie tried to prevent him from doing so by jumping on his back. Everything seemed to happen in a flash. As the other detective grabbed Marjorie, the detective bending down had by now retrieved the object, being a toffee sweet in the same sweet wrapping as those Mary and Angela had shared with them as being the sweets that the poisoned customers had eaten.

The detectives turned to Marjorie and informed her that she was being arrested. As they led her out, she was snarling and screaming that her tea shop was the best and just who did these newcomers think they were, but she had shown them. The detectives gently placed her in the squad car as onlookers, including Ken, Angela, and Mary, looked on in horror and disbelief.

Marjorie was formally charged, as at the station she made a full confession. However, upon review it was considered that she was not of sound mind and a formal application was made for her to be referred to mental health practitioners, to ensure she received appropriate treatment.

Colin and Jake were horrified when told the full story and how apparently Marjorie had previously had a mental breakdown when she and her husband, Charlie, were living and working in London. They were also very much relieved that the truth had come out and they were completely exonerated.

Both Angela and Mary's tea shops continued to flourish and the two of them actually became good friends, no doubt united by the same experience.

Ken now had attentive listeners when they visited his shop, as they were keen to know what had happened and Ken was oh, so very happy to share all the juicy details.

Marjorie's Teacosy was put up for sale by her husband Charlie, who, while for years had left her to run the shop and everything that went with that responsibility, now devoted his time to looking after her and making sure she had the right professional care and support in place for her to fully recover.

The empty shop had a few interested parties, one of which was a gentleman with a chain of flower shops. On hearing this possibility, being the generous souls they were, both Colin and Jake welcomed the potential competition, or would they?